W9-AET-847

For my mother,
who taught me to see
what is beautiful, and
my father, who showed
me the joy of giving
−GL

for Kirsty, with love
−GH

tiger tales
an imprint of ME Media, LLC
202 Old Ridgefield Road, Wilton, CT 06897
Published in the United States 2004
Originally published in Great Britain 2003
By Little Tiger Press
An imprint of Magi Publications
Text ©2003 Gillian Lobel
Illustrations ©2003 Gaby Hansen
CIP data is available
ISBN 1-58925-034-6
Printed in Singapore
1 3 5 7 9 10 8 6 4 2

LITTLE BEAR'S SPECIAL WISH

by GILLIAN LOBEL

Illustrated by
GABY HANSEN

tiger tales

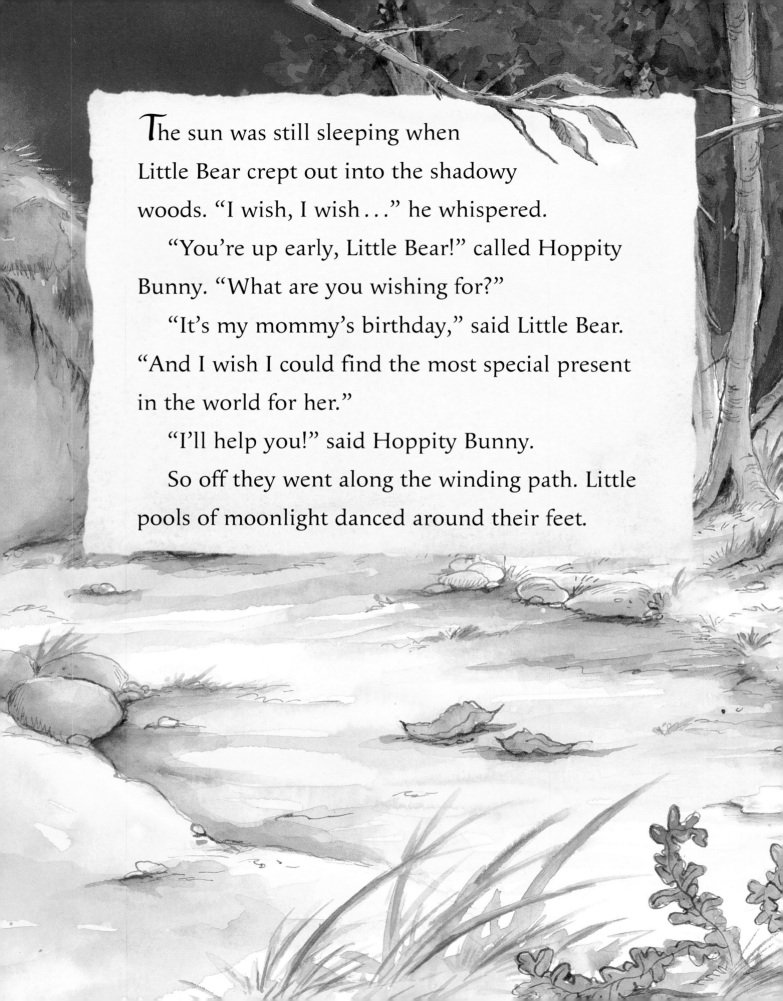

The sun was still sleeping when Little Bear crept out into the shadowy woods. "I wish, I wish..." he whispered.

"You're up early, Little Bear!" called Hoppity Bunny. "What are you wishing for?"

"It's my mommy's birthday," said Little Bear. "And I wish I could find the most special present in the world for her."

"I'll help you!" said Hoppity Bunny.

So off they went along the winding path. Little pools of moonlight danced around their feet.

In the middle of the woods was a big rock.
Little Bear sat down for a minute to think. High
above him glittered a star, so big and bright he
could almost touch it.

"I know! I could give my mommy a star," he
said. "That would be a very special present."

Little Bear gave a little jump. But he could not reach the star.

He gave a very big jump. But still he could not reach the star. Then Little Bear had an idea.

"I know!" he said. "If we climb to the very top of the hill, then we will be able to reach the stars!"

From the top of the hill the stars looked even brighter—and much closer, too. Little Bear stretched up onto his tiptoes. But the stars were still too far away. Then Little Bear had an even better idea.

"I know what we can do!" he said. "We can build a big, big tower to the stars!"

"I'll help you!" said Hoppity Bunny.

Together they piled the biggest stones they could find, one on top of the other. Then they stepped back and looked. A stone stairway stretched to the stars.

"Now I can reach a star for my mommy," said Little Bear happily. He climbed right to the top and stretched out a paw.

But still he could not reach the stars.

"I have an idea!" said Hoppity Bunny. "If I climb onto your shoulders, then I can knock a star out of the sky with my long ears!"

Hoppity Bunny scrambled up to Little Bear's shoulders. He stretched his long ears up to the sky. He waved his ears furiously.

"Be careful, Hoppity!" called Little Bear. "You're making me wobble!"

Suddenly Little Bear felt someone tapping on his foot. "Can I help you?" croaked a voice.

"Yes, I think you can, Green Frog," said Little Bear. "Aren't you a good jumper?"

Green Frog puffed out his chest. "Just watch me!" he said. High into the air he leaped, and landed right between Hoppity Bunny's long ears.

"Can you reach the brightest star from there?" asked Little Bear.

"No problem!" shouted Green Frog. He took a deep breath. "Look out, stars!" he shouted. "Here I come!"

Green Frog gave a great push with his strong
back legs. Up, up, up he sailed. Hoppity Bunny's
long ears twirled around and around.

"Help!" he shouted. "Somebody save me!"

Backward and forward swayed Hoppity, and
backward and forward swayed Little Bear. With
a mighty crash the stone tower toppled to the
ground, and down tumbled Hoppity Bunny
and Little Bear.

"I can't breathe!" gasped Little Bear. "You're sitting right on my nose!"

Then Green Frog sailed down from the sky and landed on Hoppity Bunny's head.

"I'm sorry Little Bear," he said. "I jumped right over the moon, but I still could not reach the stars."

Little Bear sat up carefully. His nose was scratched and his head hurt. "My special wish will never come true," he said. "I'll never find a star for my mommy."

"Don't be sad, Little Bear," said Hoppity Bunny. And he gave Little Bear a big hug.

A tear ran down Little Bear's nose and splashed into a tiny puddle at his feet.

As Little Bear rubbed his eyes, he saw something dancing and sparkling in the tiny puddle. It must be his star!

Little Bear jumped up with excitement. "I know what I can do to get a star!" he cried.

Off he ran down the hillside. "Wait for us!" cried Hoppity Bunny and Green Frog.

They all ran through the woods and across the
dewy meadow until they reached the stream, silvery
in the moonlight. For a long time they searched along
the sandy shore until Little Bear found just what
he was looking for. Then, very carefully, he
carried this special thing all the way home.

"Happy Birthday, Mommy!" cried Little Bear.

He placed a pearly shell that shone like a rainbow into his mother's lap. In the heart of the shell, a tiny pool of water quivered. And in that pool a very special star shimmered and shook—the star that had made a little bear's birthday wish come true.

"Hoppity Bunny and Green Frog helped me find the shell, but I caught the star all by myself!" said Little Bear proudly.

Mommy Bear knelt down and gave Little Bear a big hug.

"Thank you all very much," she said. "This is a very special birthday present."